For my daughter, Nicola
—K.A.

http://www.randomhouse.com/
ISBN: 0-679-88409-2
Library of Congress Catalog Card Number: 96-071575
LIFE FAVORS is a trademark of Random House, Inc.
Printed in the United States of America   10   9 8 7 6 5 4 3 2 1

BEST FRIENDS

PHOTOGRAPHS BY

Kim Anderson

WRITTEN BY *Heather Lowenberg*

LIFE FAVORS™

Random House 🏠 New York

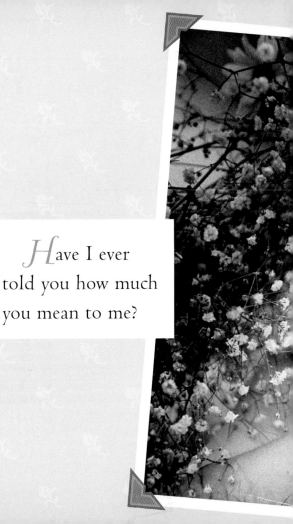

*H*ave I ever
told you how much
you mean to me?

We've been best friends for so many years. Laughing through good times and sharing the tears.

γou've always known
the right words to say.
Somehow you make
all the clouds go away.

I often think of the fun that we've had.
Singing and dancing in warm summer showers...

Walking through fields of sweet-smelling flowers.

*I*ce-cream treats
on hot summer days...
cozy naps under
the sun's bright rays.

Remember shopping for our favorite things? Fancy hats, party shoes, and friendship rings!

Wherever we were,
whatever we'd do—
we'd always be the
inseparable two.

The secrets we share
will never be told.
They're kept safe and
sound, no matter how old.

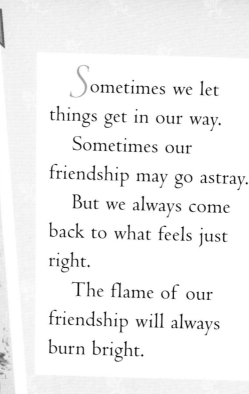

Sometimes we let things get in our way.

Sometimes our friendship may go astray.

But we always come back to what feels just right.

The flame of our friendship will always burn bright.

Good friends are special and so hard to find.

Your trust and support make *you* the best kind.

From the first
day we met, I knew
it was true.

There's simply
no one else quite
like you.

We stand together
in every endeavor.
Best friends always,
now and *forever*.